JEWEL STICKER STORIES

Kermit's Christmas Tree

By Sonali Fry
Illustrated by Larry DiFiori

For John, Beth, Monica, and Julia Elise—L.D.

MUPPET PRESS
Grosset & Dunlap • New York

ISBN 0-448-42404-5   A B C D E F G H I J

Tonight was Kermit's big Christmas party. His Muppet friends would be coming, and he and his nephew, Robin, were almost finished with the preparations.

"Okay, Robin," said Kermit. "Now all we need is a Christmas tree. Let's head over to Gonzo's new Trees and Trumpets store. I'm sure he'll have a great selection."

Put a jewel sticker on the prettiest present.

Kermit took out his sled. "I'll give you
a ride to Gonzo's, and then we'll use the
sled to carry the tree home," said Kermit.

Want to make Kermit's sled sparkle?
Put a jewel sticker on it!

"Can *I* pick out the tree,
Uncle Kermit?" asked Robin.
"Of course you can," said
Kermit.

Once they got to Gonzo's store, Robin examined every tree. It was hard to find one that was just right. They were either too crooked, too big, too little, or too, too *something!*

GONZO'S
TREES
&
TRUMPETS

Finally, Robin stopped in front of one. "What do you think about this tree, Uncle Kermit?" he asked.

"Looks good to me, Robin," said Kermit. "Let's take it."

Gonzo helped tie the tree to the sled.

"See you at the party tonight," said Robin.

"Right after I close up," Gonzo promised.

Which tree would *you* pick?
Mark it with a jewel sticker.

On their way home, Kermit and Robin bumped into Miss Piggy.

"Oh, Kermie," she cooed, "why don't you and Robin come inside and have a yummy cup of hot chocolate with me?"

Place a jewel sticker on Miss Piggy's fancy hat.

"Thanks, Piggy," said Kermit, "but we need to get this tree home. We want to decorate it before our party tonight. You'll be there, won't you?"

"Of course! I'd never miss *your* party, Kermie," said Miss Piggy, fluttering her lashes.

As soon as Kermit and Robin got home, they placed the tree in the stand.

"Oh no!" cried Robin. "This tree is much too short, Uncle Kermit!"

"Well...yes, it is a bit short," admitted Kermit.

Robin looked like he might cry. "We *have* to have a taller tree," he said.

"Don't worry, Robin," said Kermit. "Let's go back to Gonzo's and see if he has one."

Oops! Robin has dropped his mitten. Mark it with a jewel sticker.

Kermit and Robin hurried back to Gonzo's and exchanged the tree. On the way home, they saw Rizzo at his new snow cone stand.

"Get your fresh snow cones here. Cherry, lemon, or tuna fish! Come on, guys," Rizzo shouted. "What's better on a cold day than an icy cold snow cone?"

"Sorry, Rizzo," said Kermit, "but Robin and I need to get this tree decorated before the party tonight. You're coming, right?"

"Sure! Wouldn't miss it!" said Rizzo.

Put a jewel sticker on
Rizzo's snow cone sign!

Kermit and Robin carried the tree inside and
tried to put it in the stand. But the tree was too tall—
much, much too tall.

"Oh, no!" cried Robin. "What are we going to do?
We won't have a tree for our Christmas party!"

Kermit looked at the clock. "Hmmm...Gonzo's store closes soon. We might still have time to get another tree, but we'll really have to hurry!"

Put a jewel sticker on Kermit's clock.

Kermit and Robin raced back to Gonzo's store. They were so out of breath they could hardly speak. Gonzo was closing up.

"Gonzo, wait!" gasped Kermit. "This tree is too big!"

"Well, I have only one tree left," he said. "If you want it, it's yours."

"Uncle Kermit, it's perfect!" said Robin. "I guess I didn't see it before."

"We'll take it," said Kermit. "Thanks again, Gonzo."

Put a jewel sticker on Gonzo's sign.

Kermit and Robin brought the new tree inside and set it in the stand.

It wasn't too tall, and it wasn't too short. It was just right.

"Good job, Robin," said Kermit. "You found the perfect tree."

Place a jewel sticker on the tree.

Now all they needed were the Christmas tree decorations. Robin went up to the attic for them...

An ornament has rolled away.
Put a jewel sticker on it.

and passed them to his Uncle Kermit.

But before they could decorate the tree, the doorbell rang. It was Miss Piggy, Gonzo, Rizzo, and Fozzie.

"Bet you didn't know this was a tree-trimming party!" said Kermit.

Add a jewel sticker to Gonzo's trumpet.

"Oh, Kermie! What a perfect tree!" said Miss Piggy. "And you know what? It reminds me of *moi*—not too tall, and not too short, but just right."

Uh-oh! Gonzo is tangled in the lights. Mark them with jewel stickers.

Merry Christmas, everyone!

**Use the rest of your jewel stickers
to decorate Kermit's Christmas tree.**